First published by Parragon in 2011

Parragon
Queen Street House
4 Queen Street
Bath BA1 1HE, UK

Lady and the TRAMP

Adaptation by Debbie Weiss

Bath • New York • Singapore • Hong Kong • Cologne • Delhi
Melbourne • Amsterdam • Johannesburg • Auckland • Shenzhen

Lady lived very happily with her owners, Darling and Jim Dear. When Lady grew up, Jim Dear and Darling gave her a collar with a name tag. Lady proudly showed her collar to her friends Jock and Trusty.

"She's a full-grown lady," said Jock.

Tramp was another dog who was sometimes in the neighborhood. He didn't have a warm home and family. He wandered the streets, looking for scraps and helping his friends escape the dogcatcher.

One day, Tramp overheard Jock and Trusty telling
Lady that Jim Dear and Darling were expecting a baby.
"What's a baby?" Lady asked.
"A home wrecker, that's what," said
Tramp. Lady's happy life was
about to change.

When Jim Dear and Darling decided to take a trip, Aunt Sarah came to look after the baby. Her two Siamese cats came, too. Aunt Sarah was not very nice to Lady.

Her two cats were not very nice, either. They made a mess of the house and pretended that Lady caused the trouble.

"Oh, that wicked animal!" said Aunt Sarah.

Aunt Sarah took Lady straight to the pet store.
"I want a good, strong muzzle," Aunt Sarah said.
The muzzle scared Lady. She jumped off the counter and ran out the door, not knowing where she was going.

She ran and ran. Soon some big, mean dogs started to chase after her. Lady was scared, and ran into an alley. Luckily, Tramp heard all the barking and raced to Lady's rescue.

"Oh, poor kid," said Tramp, looking at Lady's muzzle. "We've gotta get this thing off. Come on."

Tramp took Lady to the zoo; maybe one of the animals could help Lady.

The apes, the alligator, and the hyena were no help at all.
Then Lady and Tramp found the beaver. He loved to chew and
soon bit right through the muzzle strap.

"It's off!" Lady said with relief.

The beaver was happy too. He could use the muzzle as a handy-dandy log puller.

Lady and Tramp thanked the beaver, and left the zoo together.

Then Tramp took Lady to supper at Tony's Restaurant. Tramp's friend Tony liked Lady and fed the pair his speciality— spaghetti with meatballs!

Tramp and Lady accidentally ate the same spaghetti noodle. The next thing they knew, they were kissing! Lady and Tramp were falling in love, and they went to watch the moon rise over the city.

The next morning, on the way home, Tramp and Lady passed a chicken coop.

"Ever chased chickens?" Tramp asked. He couldn't resist.

Lady did not like the idea, but she followed him anyway. The chickens ran around the yard squawking and squealing.

"Hey, what's going on in there?" the farmer called.

Lady and Tramp ran away as fast as they could. But Tramp soon discovered that Lady wasn't behind him. She had run into the dogcatcher and was taken to the dog pound!

Lady was scared to be at the dog pound. But soon the dogcatcher came for her. Reading her collar, he knew where to take her.

"You're too nice a girl to be in this place," he said and returned Lady to Aunt Sarah.

At home, Aunt Sarah chained Lady to the doghouse. Lady was so sad, even Jock and Trusty could not cheer her up.

Then Tramp arrived. Lady was angry with him. She thought Tramp had only looked out for himself and had let her get caught.

He tried to explain. "I thought you were right behind me, honest," he said.

"Good-bye. And take this with you," Lady said, returning the bone Tramp had brought for her.

Just then, Lady saw a rat creeping into the baby's room.
She couldn't chase it because of the chain. She could only bark.
"Stop that!" Aunt Sarah called. "Hush."

But Tramp heard and rushed back to Lady.

"What is it?" Tramp asked.

"A rat in the baby's room," Lady replied.

Tramp ran into the house and saw the rat. He had to catch
that rat before it hurt the baby.

Meanwhile, Lady was barking with all her might and pulling on the heavy chain. At last the chain broke free from the doghouse. Lady ran inside to help Tramp.

Tramp chased the rat under the baby's cot and accidentally knocked it over. The baby started to cry. But Lady was happy because the baby was safe—Tramp had finally caught the rat.

Aunt Sarah was not happy. The baby's crying woke her, and she found Lady and Tramp in his room. She thought they were hurting the baby. She called the dogcatcher to come for Tramp.

The dogcatcher soon arrived and put Tramp in his wagon.

Just then, Jim Dear and Darling came home. Lady tried to explain what happened. She lifted the curtain to show that Tramp had caught the rat and saved the baby.

Jock and Trusty had a plan to stop the dogcatcher's wagon. They barked loudly, scaring the horses. The wagon crashed, and Tramp was safe.

Jim Dear and Lady found him and took him back to their home.

The next Christmas Eve, Jock and Trusty came by to see Lady, Tramp—and their four new puppies.

"They've got their mother's eyes," said Trusty.

"There's a bit of their father in them, too," said Jock, watching a mischevious little grey puppy.

Everyone was happy that Tramp had become part of the family.

The End

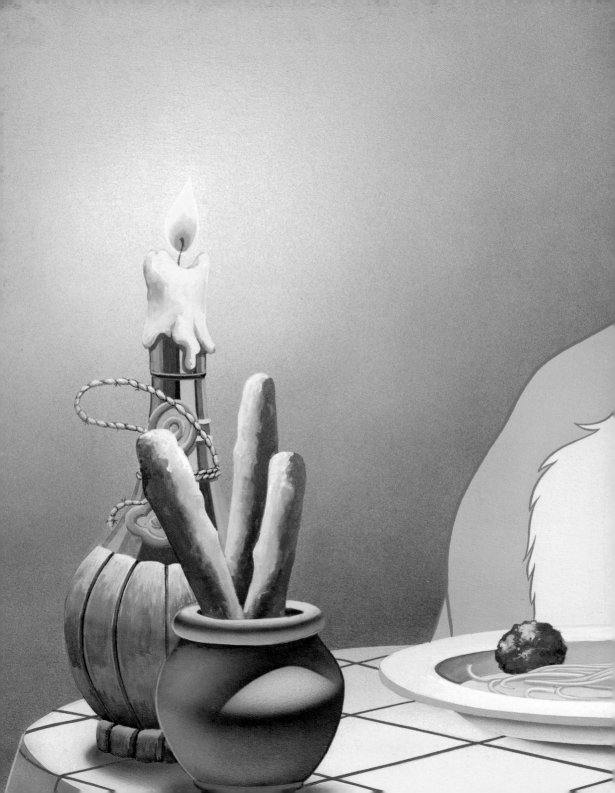